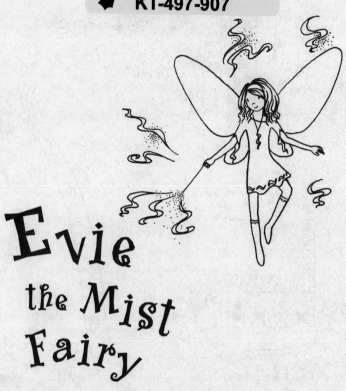

Evie the Mist Fairy

by Daisy Meadows

illustrated by Georgie Ripper

Join the Rainbow Magic Reading Challenge!

Read the story and collect your fairy points to climb the Reading Rainbow online. Turn to the back of the book for details!

This book is worth 5 points.

The Weather Fairies

Thanks to real fairies everywhere

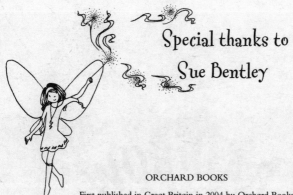

Special thanks to
Sue Bentley

ORCHARD BOOKS

First published in Great Britain in 2004 by Orchard Books
This edition published in 2016 by The Watts Publishing Group

3 5 7 9 10 8 6 4 2

© 2016 Rainbow Magic Limited.
© 2016 HIT Entertainment Limited.
Illustrations © Georgie Ripper 2004

HiT entertainment

A CIP catalogue record for this book is available from the British Library.

ISBN 978 1 40834 862 8

Printed in Great Britain

MIX
Paper from
responsible sources
FSC® C104740

FSC
www.fsc.org

The paper and board used in this book are made from wood from responsible sources

Orchard Books
An imprint of Hachette Children's Group
Part of The Watts Publishing Group Limited
Carmelite House, 50 Victoria Embankment, London EC4Y 0DZ

An Hachette UK Company
www.hachette.co.uk
www.hachettechildrens.co.uk

Goblins green and goblins small,
I cast this spell to make you tall.
As high as the palace you shall grow.
My icy magic makes it so.

Then steal Doodle's magic feathers,
Used by the fairies to make all weathers.
Climate chaos I have planned
On Earth, and here, in Fairyland!

Contents

A Misty Morning

"Wake up, sleepy head!" cried Kirsty Tate to her friend, Rachel, as she jumped out of bed and started to dress.

Rachel Walker was asleep in the spare bed in Kirsty's room. She was staying with Kirsty and her parents in the village of Wetherbury. Sleepily, she rolled over and opened her eyes. "I was dreaming that we were back in Fairyland," she told Kirsty. "The weather was topsy-turvy — sunny and snowing all at the same time — and Doodle was trying to sort it out." Doodle, the fairies' magic weather cockerel, had been on Rachel's mind a lot lately, because she and Kirsty were on an important fairy mission!

Each day in Fairyland, with the help
of the Weather Fairies, Doodle used
his magic tail feathers to organise the
weather. Each of the seven magic
feathers controlled a different kind of
weather, and each of the seven Weather
Fairies was responsible for working with
one feather in particular. The system
worked perfectly until mean old Jack
Frost sent seven goblins to steal Doodle's
magic feathers.

The goblins ran off into the human
world with one feather each, and when
poor Doodle followed them out of
Fairyland, he found himself transformed
into a rusty metal weather-vane. The
Queen of the Fairies had asked Rachel
and Kirsty to help find the magic
feathers and return them to Doodle.

Meanwhile, Fairyland's weather was all mixed up – and the goblins had been using the feathers to cause weather chaos in the human world too.

"Poor Doodle," Kirsty said, looking out of the window at the old barn where the cockerel was perched. Her dad had found Doodle lying in the park, and thinking he was an ordinary weather-vane, Mr Tate had brought him home and put him on the barn roof.

"Hopefully we'll find another magic feather today," Kirsty continued. "We've already found four of the stolen feathers. We just need to find the other three and then Doodle will get his magic back."

"Yes," Rachel agreed, brightening at the thought. "But I have to go home in three days, so we don't have long!" As she gazed out at the blue sky, a wisp of silvery mist caught her eye. "Look, that cloud is shaped just like a feather!" she said.

Kirsty looked where Rachel was pointing. "I can't see anything."

Rachel looked again. The wispy shape had vanished. "Perhaps I imagined it," she sighed, turning away to dress.

The memory of the dream fizzed in her tummy like lemonade bubbles.

It felt like a magical start to the day.

She loved staying with Kirsty and sharing fairy adventures with her. The girls had met whilst on holiday on Rainspell Island with their parents.

That was when they had first helped the fairies. On that occasion, Jack Frost had cast a nasty spell to banish the Rainbow Fairies from Fairyland, and the girls had helped all seven of them get safely home.

Rachel and Kirsty hurried down to the kitchen. Mr Tate was sitting at the table. He looked up and smiled at the girls. "Did you sleep well?"

"Yes, thanks," Rachel replied. As she
sat down, she saw a bright green notice
on the kitchen table. It read, Grand Fun
Run at Green Wood Forest, Wetherbury.
Everyone welcome. She looked at the date.
"That's today."

"Yes. Mum's running in it," said Kirsty.

"Most of the village is taking part.
Why don't you two go and watch?"
suggested Mr Tate. "You could give
Mum some moral support."

"OK," Rachel and Kirsty agreed happily.

Maybe we could look for goblins on the way, thought Rachel. She felt excited, and a bit nervous. Goblins were nasty, tricky things and Jack Frost had cast a spell to make them bigger than normal. Thankfully, fairy law states that nothing can be taller than the King and Queen's fairy castle, so the goblins couldn't get too big. But they still stood nearly as high as Rachel and Kirsty's shoulders.

Mr Tate finished his cup of tea and stood up. "I'm going to pick up Gran and take her to watch the fun run. We might see you there," he told the girls.

"OK, Dad. Goodbye," Kirsty said with a wave.

Just then, Mrs Tate dashed into the kitchen, wearing her jogging kit of shorts, T-shirt and trainers. She smiled at

Kirsty and Rachel.
"Sorry, I can't stop,
girls. I promised to
help mark out the
course in the forest."

"That's all right,
Mum. We'll follow
you up there," Kirsty said.

"We're coming to cheer you on,"
Rachel explained.

"See you at the woods then!" Mrs Tate
called cheerfully as she disappeared out
of the door.

A little later, Kirsty and Rachel set out
for Green Wood Forest themselves.

"Let's take the river path," Kirsty suggested.
"It's a bit longer, but it's much prettier."

"Oh, yes, we might see some ducklings,"
Rachel agreed eagerly.

As the girls walked up Twisty Lane, sunlight poured through the dancing tree branches and spots of light speckled the road like golden coins. Soon they reached the river. It was very pretty down by the water, where cheerful buttercups dotted the grass and cows grazed happily.

Rachel spotted little puffs of mist rising from the water. "Look! Do you think that could be fairy mist?" she asked.

"I'm not sure," Kirsty replied. "There's often mist round water, isn't there?"

"Oh, yes, especially in the morning and the evening," Rachel remembered. She felt a little disappointed, but brightened when she saw two swans gliding past, followed by three young cygnets. Dragonflies with gossamer wings perched in the reeds beside the sparkling river. "It's a perfect day!" she remarked.

Kirsty nodded. Just ahead she could see the start of the forest. Something was shimmering on a branch of one of the nearer trees. It looked like a ragged silver-grey shawl, glimmering softly in the sunlight.

"What's that?" she asked Rachel.

Rachel went over to have a look. "I don't know, but it's lovely!" she replied. "Just like angel hair for decorating trees at Christmas."

"There's lots more of it on the other branches. Isn't it pretty?" Kirsty touched a strand of the strange, silvery stuff. It clung to her fingers for a moment, before melting away. "It feels cold!" Kirsty shivered, rubbing her hands together.

Rachel leaned forward for a closer look. Tiny silvery lights shimmered among the fine, silky threads. "I'm sure this is fairy mist," she whispered excitedly.

Kirsty's eyes lit up. "I think you're right," she agreed. She looked towards a clump of tall oaks. A wispy cloud of the strange sparkly mist was building in the sky and floating gently down towards the trees. "More fairy mist!" Kirsty pointed out. "Come on!"

Magic in the Mist

The girls ran towards a stile that led into the wood. They were out of breath by the time they jumped down onto the forest path and looked around. Wispy, silver mist clung to trees everywhere and coated the grass with tiny droplets. Every twig, leaf and flower glowed and shimmered with a soft silver light.

And where the sunbeams reached down through the trees, the fairy mist sparkled with rainbow light.

"Oh!" breathed Rachel. "It's so beautiful!"

Kirsty stared open-mouthed at the forest. It looked almost as magical as Fairyland itself!

Slowly, the girls moved forward.

After a few steps, Rachel realised that she couldn't see very far ahead.

"This mist is building up fast," she said. "The goblin with the Mist Feather must be hiding really nearby."

Kirsty nodded as thick fog swirled around them. "You're right, Rachel," she agreed. "And we can hardly see a thing. The goblin could be right behind us!"

Rachel rubbed her bare arms and shivered nervously. Only a couple of minutes had passed, but as the mist grew thicker, the forest began to feel dark and unfriendly. Nothing glittered or gleamed anymore. The fog was settling around the girls like a cold blanket.

Shadowy figures moved up ahead. A man wearing a red T-shirt ran out in front of the girls as another runner burst out of the trees. They were heading straight for each other. "Watch out!" called Kirsty. But it was too late. Crash! The runners bumped into each other.

"Sorry. Didn't see you there!" one
of them said, rubbing his head.

"I've never seen fog like this in
summer," replied the other one.

Rachel and Kirsty could hear rustles
and bumps all round them. Complaining
voices echoed through the fog. Lots of
runners were getting lost and having
to walk in order to avoid the trees.

"What a shame. This fog is ruining the fun run," said Rachel.

The fog still seemed to be getting thicker. It cloaked the trees in robes of dull grey, making them look dark and sinister.

Suddenly, something caught Kirsty's eye. "Over there!" she pointed.

A bright light was moving towards them, shining like a lantern. Soon the girls could see that it was a tiny gleaming fairy.

"Oh!" gasped Kirsty. "It's Evie the Mist Fairy!"

"Hello again, Rachel and Kirsty," cried Evie in a bright, tinkly voice, as she hovered in the air in front of them. The girls had met Evie in Fairyland, along with all the other Weather Fairies. She had long dark hair and violet eyes. She wore a floaty lilac dress with purple boots, and her wand had a sparkly silver tip from which wisps of shimmering mist drifted constantly.

"Oh, we're so glad to see you!" said Rachel delightedly.

"We really need your help," Kirsty added. "We're sure that the goblin with the Mist Feather isn't far away."

"Yes!" agreed Evie, a frown on her tiny face. "And he's causing lots of misty mischief!"

"Could you leave a magic trail behind us, as we go further into the woods?" Rachel asked. "Then we can look for the goblin and still find our way back to the stile and out."

Evie grinned. She waved her wand and a fountain of fairy dust shot out. It floated to the ground and formed a glittering path. "Of course, now we won't get lost!" she said. "But we might bump into the runners," Kirsty pointed out. "Let's turn ourselves into fairies, Rachel, then we can fly."

The Fairy Queen
had given Rachel
and Kirsty
beautiful golden
lockets full of
fairy dust. The
girls sprinkled
themselves with
the magic dust and
soon shrank to
fairy size. The trees
seemed as big as
giants' castles looming
out of the thick fog.

"I love being a fairy!" Kirsty sang
out happily.

Rachel twisted round to look over her
shoulder. There were her fairy wings on
her back, shining and delicate.

"Hooray!" Evie rose into the air, a
trail of glittering mist streaming from
her wand, and the two girls followed
her deeper into the forest.

Below them, the runners were still stumbling about in the fog. "Poor Mum. She was really looking forward to today. That nasty goblin's spoiling everyone's fun," said Kirsty crossly.

Suddenly, Rachel spotted a dark, hunched shape in the mist below. She waved urgently to Kirsty and Evie. "Look down there," she called softly. "I think we've found the goblin!"

Goblin in the Fog

They all floated down to investigate.
The mist was heavier here and sticky. It
dragged at Rachel's wings as she flew
through it. "Oh, it's not a goblin – it's
just a dead tree," she sighed, landing
on the thick twisted trunk. She felt
disappointed. The dark, squat shape had
looked just like a goblin from the air.

"We may not have found him yet," Kirsty whispered to her friend, "but I still think that goblin's nearby. The mist here smells nasty and musty and it's harder to fly through."

Rachel fluttered her beautiful shiny wings. "Yes," she agreed. "It's like cold porridge."

Just then, they heard a gruff, complaining voice. "It's not fair! I'm cold and I'm lost and I'm hungry!" There was a loud sniff, like a pig snorting. "Poor me!"

Rachel, Kirsty, and Evie looked at each other in excitement.

"That's definitely a goblin speaking!"
declared Evie.

"Quick! Let's hide in that tree before he
sees us," suggested Rachel.

They flew upwards to land
on the branch of a huge
oak and peered down
through the thick
green leaves. Sure
enough, the goblin
sat on a log below
them. They could
see the top of his
head and his
enormous bony feet.
They could also hear
a horrible gurgling
sound, like slimy stuff
going down a plughole.

"Lost in this horrible forest! And I'm so hungry," moaned the goblin, clutching his rumbling tummy. "I'd love some toadstool stew and worm dumplings!" Suddenly he jumped up.

"What was that? Who's there?" He peered up into the tree's branches. Rachel, Kirsty and Evie quickly darted behind the oak leaves and after a moment the goblin sank down onto his log again. "Must have been a squirrel," he muttered. "I want to go home!"

The girls could see the goblin clearly now. He had bulging, crossed eyes and a big, lumpy nose like a potato.

His arms were long and skinny but he
had short legs and knobbly knees.

"Look what he's holding!" whispered
Evie.

Kirsty and Rachel peered through the
leaves and saw that a beautiful silvery
feather with a lilac tip was clutched in
the goblin's stubby fingers. "The Mist
Feather!" the girls exclaimed together.

Then Rachel frowned. "If the goblin's lost in the fog, why doesn't he use the magic feather to get rid of it?" she asked.

"Because he doesn't know how," Evie explained. "He's waving the feather about all over the place without thinking – but by doing so he's only making more and more mist."

It was true. The goblin was shaking the Mist Feather and mumbling to himself sorrowfully as thick swirls of fog drifted around him. "Earwig fritters, beetle pancakes, lovely slug sandwiches…" he muttered.

40

Just then, one of the runners passed close by. The goblin shot to his feet and hid behind a tree. He was trembling so much that the three friends could hear his knees knocking together. "It's a…it's a Pogwurzel!" he whispered in panic.

As the sound of the runner's footsteps faded, the goblin peeped out. "Phew! The Pogwurzel's gone." He flopped back down on the log, but kept on looking about him nervously.

Kirsty turned to Evie. "What is a Pogwurzel?" she asked.

Evie smiled, her violet eyes sparkling. "Pogwurzels are strange, terrible magical, goblin-chasing monsters!" she replied.

Rachel looked at the fairy curiously. "Where do they live?" She and Kirsty had been to Fairyland a few times now. They had seen elves, goblins and all kinds of fairies – but never a Pogwurzel.

Evie gave a peal of silvery laughter. "Nowhere!" she said. "Because they don't exist! You see goblin children can be really naughty, so their mothers tell them that if they don't do as they're told, a Pogwurzel will come and chase them!"

Kirsty and Rachel laughed so much they nearly fell off the branch.

Then Rachel suddenly turned to Kirsty and Evie in excitement. "I've got an idea," she whispered, her eyes shining. "I think I know how we can get the Mist Feather back!"

The Pogwurzel Plot

Evie and Kirsty stared at Rachel. "Tell us!" they pleaded.

Rachel outlined her plan. "If we can convince the goblin that the forest is full of Pogwurzels, he'll do anything to escape. He's bound to want the mist cleared away, so he can find his way out of the wood.

Since he's too stupid to work out how to use the Mist Feather to clear the fog, maybe we can persuade him to give the feather to Evie and let her try."

Evie clapped her hands together in delight. "Then I can keep it and take it back to Doodle!" she said. "It's a brilliant plan!"

"But I'm not sure how we can make the goblin think that there are hundreds of Pogwurzels in the forest," Rachel added.

The three friends racked their brains. Kirsty thought of her mum and the other runners trying to find their way around the fun run course. That gave her an idea of her own. "I know just how we can convince the goblin about Pogwurzels," she cried. "Evie, if you make us human-sized again, Rachel and I can creep up on the goblin from behind, then run past him, screaming that a Pogwurzel is chasing us!"

"Yes, that could work," Evie agreed.

"We'll have to be very convincing," Rachel put in.

Evie nodded. "But you two can do it.
I know you can," she said encouragingly.
The three friends flew silently down to
the ground behind the oak tree. Evie
waved her wand and the
girls zoomed up to
their normal height.
"Ready?" asked Kirsty.
"You bet," Rachel
replied firmly.
The girls crept
towards the goblin.
They could see
him sitting on
his log, still
muttering to himself.
"Now!" hissed Rachel.
Kirsty dashed forward. "Help! Help! Save
us from the Pogwurzel!" she shouted.

Rachel ran after her. "It's huge and scary and won't leave us alone!" she cried.

The goblin leapt to his feet, his eyes like saucers. "What?" he gasped. "Who are you?"

Kirsty stopped. "Oh, my goodness, a goblin in Pogwurzel Wood!" she exclaimed, pretending to be surprised.

Rachel stopped too. "You must be very brave," she declared.

The goblin's crossed-eyes flicked from Rachel to Kirsty. "Why?" he demanded shakily. "Are their many Pogwurzels around here?"

"Oh, yes," Kirsty chimed in. "Hundreds. This forest is full of them. One of them was chasing us just now," she added, looking nervously over her shoulder. "He'll be along soon I should think."

Just then, Evie fluttered down, her wings shining in the fog. "Pogwurzels especially love to catch goblins, you know. I've heard that they cook them and eat them," she said.

"Eat them!" the
goblin's face
turned pale
with fear.

"Oh, yes.
If I was you,
I'd get out of
this wood right
now," Evie went on.

"But I can't," wailed the goblin. "I've
lost my way. The fog is so thick I can
hardly see my own bony toes!"

Evie smiled. "I'll help you," she said
sweetly. "Just give me that feather
you're holding and I'll magic a clear
pathway out of the forest for you."

Kirsty and Rachel hardly dared
breathe. Their plan was working so far,
but what would the goblin do next?

He pinched his nose thoughtfully. "I don't know. Jack Frost won't like it if I give you the Mist Feather."

"But he's not the one being chased by a Pogwurzel, is he?" Rachel pointed out quickly. "He's not the one who'll be roasted and toasted and turned into Goblin Pie!"

"The Pogwurzels in this wood are extra-enormous," Kirsty put in. "And really, really fierce."

"So is Jack Frost," the goblin said, looking sullen. "I think I'll keep the feather."

Kirsty's heart sank. It looked like the goblin was more stubborn than they had expected. She exchanged looks with Rachel. Now what could they do?

Goblin Pie

Evie hovered close to the girls. "I've got an idea," she whispered. "You distract the goblin, so he won't notice what I'm doing."

"What are you all talking about?" demanded the goblin suspiciously.

"We think we heard another Pogwurzel," Kirsty replied.

"Where?" the goblin spun round anxiously.

While his back was turned, Evie waved her wand in a complicated pattern. A big fountain of silver and violet sparks shot into a nearby bush, carrying fairy magic there.

"I can hear it! It's coming this way!" Rachel called to the goblin.

"Don't believe you," the goblin sneered. "I can't hear it. You're just trying to scare me. I bet you never even saw a Pogwurzel in the first place."

"Listen properly for yourself then," Evie said.

The goblin put his head on one side and frowned in concentration. Kirsty and Rachel waited. They weren't sure exactly what Evie had planned.

Suddenly a deep, scary roar came from the centre of the nearby bush.

"Raaghh! I'm a ferocious Pogwurzel!
And I really fancy Goblin
Pie for my supper!"

"Wow! Evie's magical
voice is really scary,"
Kirsty whispered
to Rachel.

The goblin
stiffened. "Help
me, Mummy!" he
cried. "A Pogwurzel
wants to eat me!
I'm sorry I put those
toenail clippings in
your bed. I won't do
it again. Help!" He
stumbled behind Kirsty and
Rachel, trying to hide. "Don't
eat me, Mr Pogwurzel. Eat these girls

instead. I bet they taste sweeter than me!" Evie's magical trick voice came from the bush again. "I only eat goblins," it boomed. "Especially really naughty ones – like you!" The goblin squealed in alarm and his eyes bulged. He took the Mist Feather from his belt and thrust it at Evie. "Make the mist go away so I can get out of here," he begged. "I don't want to be made into Goblin Pie!"

Evie gave a joyful smile, took the feather and waved it expertly in the air. A clear path immediately appeared through the mist. The goblin gave a final terrified glance over his shoulder and then ran away as fast as he could, his big feet flapping noisily.

Kirsty, Rachel and Evie laughed merrily.

"Evie, that trick voice was brilliant!" Rachel said.

"It even scared me!" laughed Kirsty.

"And now we have the Mist Feather!" Evie declared, waving it over her head.

Silver sparks shot into
the air and the mist
began to fade.
Moments later, the
sun shone down
onto the forest again.

Rachel and Kirsty beamed.
We can give another magic feather
back to Doodle!" Rachel said happily.

Evie flew up and did a little twirl in the
air for joy. Silver and violet mist
sparkled all around her.

"And the fun run should be easier
going now," Kirsty put in. "Let's go
and see if we can spot Mum before we
head home to Doodle."

Back on Course

The three friends made their way
towards the fun run course.

The bracken and forest paths were
touched with gold, and the smell of
earth and green leaves filled the air.
Runners pounded along between trees
marked with big red signs. Everyone
could see where they were going now.

"You'd better hide on my shoulder," Rachel said to Evie.

Evie nodded and fluttered beneath Rachel's hair.

Suddenly, Kirsty spotted her mum dashing through the trees. Two other runners were close on her heels.

"Come on, Mum!" Kirsty shouted.

"You can do it!" yelled Rachel.

Kirsty's mum threw them a brief smile and waved. "Not far to go now," she called.

Kirsty and Rachel jumped up and
down with delight.
Evie cheered too,
but only Rachel
could hear her
silvery voice.

"Looks like
your mum's
doing well,"
said a voice
at Kirsty's side.

"Dad! Gran! You're
here!" Kirsty exclaimed.

"Only just in time. That fog held us
up," said Mr Tate. "Strange how it's
completely disappeared now. Almost like
magic."

Rachel and Kirsty looked at each other
and smiled.

"We're going to head home now,"
Kirsty told her dad.

"Right you are," he replied. "We'll go
and wait for Mum at the finish line."

On the way home, the girls revelled
in the glorious sunshine, but Kirsty
couldn't help missing the sparkly fairy
mist just a little bit.

"Time to give Doodle his feather
back," said Rachel, as they reached
Kirsty's cottage. "I wonder if he'll speak
 to us again." Every time the
girls had returned a tail
feather, Doodle had
sprung briefly to life
and started to speak.
He'd given them part
of a message and they
were keen to hear the rest.

"I hope so," said Kirsty. She repeated what Doodle had said so far. "Beware! Jack Frost will come…"

Evie flew up to the barn roof. As she slotted the feather into place, the girls watched eagerly.

A fountain of copper and gold sparks
fizzed from Doodle's tail. The rusty old
weather-vane disappeared and in its
place blazed a fiery magic cockerel.
Doodle fluffed up his glorious feathers
and turned to stare at Rachel and
Kirsty. "If his—" he squawked. But
before he could finish the message, his
feathers turned to iron and he became
an ordinary weather-vane again.

Kirsty frowned. "Beware! Jack Frost will come if his…" she said, putting together all the words Doodle had said so far.

"Jack Frost will come if his what?" queried Rachel curiously.

Kirsty shook her head. "We'll just have to find the next feather and hope Doodle can tell us," she sighed.

Evie nodded. "It's important to know the whole message. Jack Frost is dangerous," she warned. "And now I must leave you." She hugged Rachel and Kirsty in turn. "Dear friends. Thank you for helping me."

"You're welcome," said Kirsty.

"Say hello to all our friends in
Fairyland for us," added Rachel.

"I will," Evie promised, as she
zoomed up into the brilliant blue sky.
Her wand fizzed trails of silver mist,
then she was gone.

Kirsty chuckled. "I've just remembered something the goblin said. I wonder whose toenail clippings he put in his mum's bed!" she said.

Rachel laughed happily. What an exciting day it had been and there were still two days of her holiday left!

Now it's time for Kirsty and
Rachel to help...

Storm the Lightning Fairy

Read on for a sneak peek...

"I can't believe tomorrow is my last day here," groaned Rachel Walker. She was staying for a week's holiday with her friend, Kirsty Tate, at the Tates' house in Wetherbury. The girls had had so many adventures together, they knew it was going to be difficult to say goodbye.

They were walking to the park, keen to get outside now the rain had stopped. It had been pouring down all night, but now the sun was shining.

"Put your coats on, though, won't you?" Mrs Tate had told them before they set off. "It looks quite breezy out there."

"It's been such fun, having you to stay," Kirsty told her friend. "I don't think I'll ever forget this week, will you?"

Rachel shook her head. "No way," she agreed firmly.

The two friends smiled at each other. It had been a very busy week. A snowy, windy, cloudy, sunny, misty week – thanks to Jack Frost and his naughty goblins. The goblins had stolen the seven magic tail feathers from Doodle, the Fairyland weather cockerel, and taken one each into the human world. The feathers were used by the Weather Fairies to control the weather so the goblins were stirring up all kinds of trouble!

Rachel and Kirsty were helping the Weather Fairies to get the feathers back.

Without them, Doodle was just an ordinary iron weather-vane! Kirsty's dad had found him lying in the park after he'd chased the goblins into the human world. Mr Tate had brought him home and put him on the roof of the old barn.

"Doodle's got five of his magic feathers back now. But I do hope we find the last two before you have to go home," Kirsty said, pushing open the park gates.

Rachel nodded, but before she could say anything, there was a pattering sound and raindrops started splashing down.

The girls looked up in dismay to see a huge purple storm cloud covering the sun. The sky was darkening by the second and the rain was falling more and more heavily.

"Quick!" Kirsty shouted. "Before we get soaked!"

The girls started to run, and Rachel put her hands over her head as raindrops pelted them from all sides. She could hardly see the path ahead through the sudden downpour. "Where are we going?" she yelled.

"Let's just find some shelter," Kirsty replied, grabbing Rachel's hand and pulling her along. "I'm soaked through already!"

The girls stopped under a large chestnut tree near the park entrance. The tree's wide, leafy branches gave good cover. "Great idea," shivered Rachel, trying to shake the raindrops from her coat.

But just as she said that, there was a deafening rumble of thunder, followed by an almighty FLASH! The whole sky was lit up by a blast of lightning. Kirsty and Rachel watched in alarm as a lightning bolt slammed straight into the chestnut.

"We need to get away from here quickly," Kirsty cried, jumping back in fright. "It's dangerous being under the trees in a thunder storm!"

"Wait a minute," Rachel said, staring at the branch. Rain was pouring off her shoulders but she didn't seem to notice. "Kirsty, look. The branch is *sparkling*."

And so it was. The leaves were shining a bright, glittering green, glowing against the darkness of the day...

Read Storm the Lightning Fairy to find out what adventures are in store for Kirsty and Rachel!

Meet the
Friendship Fairies

When Jack Frost steals the Friendship Fairies' magical objects, BFFs everywhere are in trouble! Can Rachel and Kirsty help save the magic of friendship?

www.rainbowmagicbooks.co.uk

Calling all parents, carers and teachers!
The Rainbow Magic fairies are here to help
your child enter the magical world of reading.
Whatever reading stage they are at, there's
a Rainbow Magic book for everyone!
Here is Lydia the Reading Fairy's guide to
supporting your child's journey at all levels.

Starting Out

(1) Our Rainbow Magic Beginner Readers are perfect for first-time readers who are just beginning to develop reading skills and confidence. Approved by teachers, they contain a full range of educational levelling, as well as lively full-colour illustrations.

Developing Readers

(2) Rainbow Magic Early Readers contain longer stories and wider vocabulary for building stamina and growing confidence. These are adaptations of our most popular Rainbow Magic stories, specially developed for younger readers in conjunction with an Early Years reading consultant, with full-colour illustrations.

Going Solo

(3) The Rainbow Magic chapter books - a mixture of series and one-off specials - contain accessible writing to encourage your child to venture into reading independently. These highly collectible and much-loved magical stories inspire a love of reading to last a lifetime.

www.rainbowmagicbooks.co.uk

"Rainbow Magic got my daughter reading chapter books. Great sparkly covers, cute fairies and traditional stories full of magic that she found impossible to put down" - Mother of Edie (6 years)

"Florence LOVES the Rainbow Magic books. She really enjoys reading now" Mother of Florence (6 years)

The Rainbow Magic Reading Challenge

Well done, fairy friend – you have completed the book!
This book was worth 5 points.

See how far you have climbed on the **Reading Rainbow**
on the Rainbow Magic website below.

The more books you read, the more points you will get,
and the closer you will be to becoming a Fairy Princess!

How to get your Reading Rainbow
1. Cut out the coin below
2. Go to the Rainbow Magic website
3. Download and print out your poster
4. Add your coin and climb up the Reading Rainbow!

There's all this and lots more at
www.rainbowmagicbooks.co.uk

You'll find activities, competitions, stories, a special
newsletter and complete profiles of all the
Rainbow Magic fairies. Find a fairy with your name!